The Greatest Well-digger in the World!

CW01560399

ISRAEL EMMANUEL

SOPHOS
S B
BOOKS

Raising the voice of Wisdom!

The Greatest Well-digger in the World!

Copyright © 2007 by Israel Emmanuel

Published by

SOPHOS Books

P.O. Box 1629

Croydon

CR9 9WW

info@sophosbooks.com

Distributed by

Books With A Mission

http://www.bwam.org

All rights reserved. No part of this publication may be reproduced, stored in a retrieval system, or transmitted in any form or by any means, mechanical, electronic, photocopying or otherwise without the prior written consent of the copyright owner.

ISBN 1-905669-10-0

Cover design by *Churchbrand UK*

Printed in the United Kingdom

To the greatest sweetheart in the world,
Linda,
and the greatest children in the world,
Destiny and Daniel.
Thank you for patiently accompanying me
on my path to Highest Joy.

Acknowledgements

It is true. No mind can imagine the things that Yahweh has prepared for those who love Him. Such is the testimony of this book. I am grateful to the Lord for the inspiration to write *The Greatest Well-digger in the World* and the assignment it is ordained to fulfil.

Special thanks to those who read the manuscript: Sister Kate, Lee James and Toyin Oladele, your comments were valuable. I am once again grateful to Pastor Hugh Osgood and Pastor Sunday Adelaja.

Thanks to my mother, Esther Olulaja and all my siblings, also to everyone who is enthusiastic about the work of *Books With A Mission*. Gabrielle and Josephine of *Blue Boost*, you are amazing!

Everyone at *His Kingdom Outreach Church*, I truly love and appreciate your passion for heaven's agenda and value your partnership on this corporate journey to *Highest Joy!*

- *Israel Emmanuel*

The angel said to Marnina,

"When you meet
The Greatest Well-digger
in the World,
he will reveal to you the
path to Highest Joy..."

1

Everyone knew the great story-teller who lived in Sychar. Not only was she beautiful in her old age, she always glowed with grace and overflowed with life. Her house, situated in the centre of town, was always visited by people both young and old. Travellers, city dwellers, traders from towns beyond, they all wanted to hear the wisdom that came from her mouth. Her stories made children laugh and adults cry—stories about love and forgiveness, courage and endurance. Her imagination was rich and her voice soothing. Yes, she was esteemed by many, particularly by her husband, a respected man in Sychar.

Marnina, was full of stories. They flowed out of her like a stream and refreshed the hearts of her listeners all the time. A tale to encourage and edify. A poem to reflect upon and gain wisdom. Stories about life and ancient beginnings. Tales of conflict and victory. Each one shared from the heart with passion and emotion.

Her most favourite story, however, is the one closest to her heart. This one was not a product of a blessed imagination; this was a story she lived. Marnina's story. She loved to tell it because she knew it so well. More than this, she wanted others to know it too. She wanted everyone everywhere to learn from her sojourn in Samaria. "The greatest stories ever told are the ones that were lived before they were told," Marnina would say. No wonder why she was the greatest story-teller in the land.

Hers is the story of a lifelong search. It started with a dream. It was initiated by a prophecy. The angel told Marnina, "When you meet The Greatest Well-digger in the World, he reveal to you the path to Highest Joy and your fortunes will turn around for good." *Who is the greatest well-digger in the world?* Marnina asked herself many a time. Where can I find him? When will I meet him? She enquired from people close to her heart. She kept searching until her strength began to fail her.

This is Marnina's story, the short version of a very long jorney, best told by Marnina, the great story-teller who lived in Sychar.

2

I was born in a small town in Samaria. Father and mother rejoiced exceedingly on my arrival because they could not have a child for the first eight years of their union. They named me Marnina for the joy that my birth brought to the family.

As much as I can remember, our home was always full of delight and happiness. Father loved mother very much, and as his first child, his only child, he loved me too, dearly. My memory is full of his touch, embrace and kisses. Mother loved me too, always carrying me around. For some reason, though, I was closer to my Father and always looked forward to his homecoming. No child should be deprived of such warmth.

"Marnina, my Rose," Father would always say, "you will one day grow to be a beautiful young woman who will bring happiness to the lives of many in Samaria." I believed him.

Every night he told me stories, mostly from the Torah. I learnt about my great heritage in the Patriarchs and the God they served. Father was a worshipper of Yahweh too; he instilled in me a love for the Creator and an abhorrence of the ancient idols of Samaria.

I must have inherited my love for story-telling from my Father. "Can I tell you a story too, Father?" I enquired one day.

"Go ahead, my daughter," Father said, encouraging me along. I proceeded to tell the imaginary tale of how two sea creatures from different ends of the great ocean met and eventually became friends. Father will listen attentively and at the end give me a rousing applause.

Over time, my stories increased. Every night Father will teach me the Torah and I will tell him a story. "You have a gift of the imagination, Marnina. You will one day share your many stories with people all over Samaria."

I never forgot that statement. I believed him because he believed in me.

For some bizarre reason, I told most of my stories to Father in the evening, when he came back from the farm. Mother loved me in her own way during the day. Every morning, she would bathe me and dress me up in clean, smart clothes, and serve me breakfast. The rest of the day was spent preparing more food, tidying the house, visiting the well at the edge of the town and sometimes the market.

"My little girl," mother once said, "you are always full of words and imagery. However, the lot of a woman in life is to silently abide with her husband and take care of his domestic affairs. Sometimes you talk too much. It is not in our custom for a woman to be so inclined."

Being just eight at the time, I did not understand what mother meant by "custom." When I asked her, she simply replied "Custom is the way things are done. Samaritan women do not talk as much as you do, Marnina!"

At least, that explained why mother was usually quiet. She was abiding by the custom of the land. I could not wait for Father to come home. A fresh story was forming in my mind, as well as an urge to ask him about the custom of Samaritan women.

That evening, after supper, Father told me about father Abraham, how Yahweh gave him a son of promise in his old age. "And you, my Rose, are a great, great, great, grand daughter of father Abraham."

That was nice to know. But I also wanted to know what "custom" meant. When I finally asked, Father had a story to tell me.

"Marnina my daughter," Father started. "Mother was right in what she explained about the custom of women in our land. It has been so for many generations. Every woman grows up with a dream to be a good wife to her husband and a good mother to his children. I love your mother so much because she has always been good to me. When we could not have a baby a year into our marriage, she felt like she was letting me down. I tried to convince her otherwise, but it was not at all easy. Month after month, year after year, my beloved became increasingly withdrawn and unhappy. She wanted to be a complete woman. She wanted us to be a complete family."

"She must have been very happy when I was born," I asked.

"You are an answer to many prayers, Marnina. Mother was always full of joy as you grew in her belly. I was happy too that my dear wife would once again be the happy person she has always been."

"But Father," I said, with a quizzical look on my face. "Why is mother not always happy these days now that we are a 'complete family'?"

Father took a deep breath as he gazed into the ceiling of the room. "Marnina, it is a long story and it has to do with the word "custom" again. Because you need to be sleep now, I will tell you a bit now and promise to explain in details later. Is that alright?"

"It's alright Father," I said, eager to hear more.

"Every family looks forward to when they will

have their first boy because the family name and inheritance goes to the male. So, even though we were all overjoyed at your birth, perhaps we were half expecting a boy. I really did not mind, to be honest. Eight years was a long time to wait for your arrival. Let me now answer the question of why Mother sometimes looks unhappy. It is now another eight years after your birth and not only has she not conceived another baby, she desperately wants to give me a boy. Don't get me wrong, your mother loves you dearly. She just wants to fit properly with tradition."

"So, when I have a brother, mother will again be happy?" I asked.

"I guess so, Marnina, even though I have tried to let her know I am not at all bothered."

"But you *should* be bothered, shouldn't you?" I queried.

"You would expect me to, but I am not, and I will tell you why another day. You've already learnt a lot for your young mind. Just remember this, that you are a special child destined for greatness."

"You will tell me the rest of the story tomorrow, Father?"

"Everything is a story to you Marnina! I promise to tell you tomorrow. Now you sleep tight and may the angels watch over you through the night."

Father kissed me on the forehead and said the

words he had said almost every night, "I love you my daughter."

"I love you Father. And thank you for the story."

"Thank you for listening." Father's smile filled the room as he quietly left the room.

3

I could not wait for Father to come back from the farm. Mother had spent all afternoon preparing his favourite meal. I watched Mother as she busied herself around the house, doing a thousand things at the same time.

"What can I do to help, Mother?" I asked, wanting to lend a hand and lessen her work.

"You can set the table for your Father. He will soon be back," Mother said, as she tasted the boiling pot of stew.

I had just placed a jug of water on the table, fresh water we had drawn from Jacob's well, when Father arrived.

"Welcome home, Father!" I ran towards him and jumped into his wide open arms.

"How are you today my Marnina?" Father asked with a smile on his face.

"I am very well, Father. I have been helping

mother prepare your dinner all day," I said, wiping off the imaginary sweat from my face.

"I am sure you have. And where is your Mother?" Father asked, putting me down and looking around the room.

"Here I am my husband. Welcome home. Dinner is ready." Mother managed a smile. She was clearly exhausted from all the hard work.

"Thank you my darling." Father gave Mother a big hug. "You should take time to rest now. I can see you have been working all day."

The evening progressed peacefully and I could not wait for Father to tell me another story. Besides, wasn't he going to explain to me why he was not sad he did not have a son yet? Is he just not concerned about Samaritan customs? Why is mother worried about not having a baby boy and Father is not? I was itching for answers.

Surely, story time arrived. I heard a bit more about Abraham and his miracle son, Isaac. But I was eager to hear the rest of the story Father had promised to tell me. "Father," I braved myself.

"Yes, my Rose," he answered.

"Tell me the truth. Would you be happier if I was a boy like Isaac?"

"Marnina, you are a very smart girl. I am sure your mind has been on this issue all day long," Father stroked my head with his strong hands. Father was right. I raised my eyebrows and smiled, acknowledging his suspicion but wanting him to continue.

"I will keep my promise to you and tell you why I am as happy as I can be. I agree that the average Samaritan man would be concerned about his sonless state, but I cannot do that. I am not allowed to be."

"What do you mean, 'I am not allowed to be'?" I cut in.

"You see," Father said, with a calm look on his face, "three days before you were born, I had a dream and in the dream I was given an important message by an angel from Yahweh about the child we were expecting ."

"An angel? What did the angel say?" I was curious.

"First, the angel instructed me to read a portion of the Torah that related to Zelophehad. And then I was told that our baby will grow to be a special person of depth and influence, someone whose mouth will be filled with much wisdom. Lastly, the angel told me to love the baby with all my heart."

"Zelo-pha?" I mumbled, trying to recall the angel's instruction and how it related to the nice things spoken about me.

"Zelophehad, my Rose." Father went on to tell me the story of Zelophehad, from the tribe of Manaseh, a man who had five daughters before he died. He had no son. After his death the daughters summoned the courage to request for their inheritance amongst their father's relatives and they got their wish sanctioned by Yahweh.

Father concluded, "It was after I read the story of Zelophehad's daughters that I suspected that the baby we were expecting would be a girl. And I was determined not to allow traditional beliefs to keep me from loving you with all my heart."

"What about mother? Did she know about the dream?" I asked.

"I narrated the dream to her two weeks after you were born because she had to recover from the birth pains. She was happy to know that Yahweh had a plan for your life."

"So why is she now unhappy?"

"Well, as I said yesterday, she would like to have another child and even though the angel has spoken concerning your great future, she still will want a boy. It will make her feel accepted in society because the people of Samaria still honour boys over girls."

My young mind tried to grasp everything Father shared that night. *I am special,* I pondered many times afterwards. Father always told me so. Even when he rebuked me, he would make sure he ends his correction by affirming me. He wanted me to grow up knowing I was a child of destiny.

As for mother, I wanted her to be happy. Before I

closed my eyes to sleep that night, I prayed to Yahweh in my little way. *Please give us a son so Mother can be happy again.* Even though I could not understand the custom, I concluded having a brother to play with would be the best thing in the world.

4

"I had a dream last night, Father!" I managed to tell him before he left for the farm one bright and sunny morning.

"My daughter, you will tell me all about it when I come back, will you?" Father said, stroking my head.

"I will, Father. I cannot wait."

Ever since Father had told me of the dream he had about me, I had become more aware of the power of dreams. From Father's stories, I learnt that Yahweh sometimes spoke to people in their sleep. Had he just spoken to me? *But I am just a child, only nine years of age,* I thought to myself. So was Joseph when he had his great dreams, I remembered from Father's evening stories.

Mother noticed my unusual quietness on the breakfast table. "What's the matter, little girl? You are not your usual self today."

"Do you believe Yahweh speaks to people,

mother?" I answered with a question of my own.

"Of course I do," said mother, looking intently into my eyes. "Did you see an angel in your sleep?"

I had some ideas of my own. I still wanted to know why the custom of the land overpowered the words of the angel Father saw in his dreams. "Yes I did, mother. But if you do believe Yahweh speaks to his people, then why are you sad because you have not yet had a baby boy? The angel in Father's dream said you should always be joyful and thankful for me, but you are not always so. Don't you believe in angels?"

Mother drew a deep breath and scratched her head, as though searching for where to start. "My little girl, I believe that Yahweh speaks to us through His messengers. He also speaks to us through the Torah. Whilst I know that you are a special child who will touch many lives, I am also aware of how society responds to us women. Greater honour is given to the male child. Even Yahweh asks for the male child to be given over to Him. I want to dedicate you to Yahweh and His service but do not know how. The place of a woman's service is faithfully beside her husband in the home. That's what I've always done and that is what society will expect you to do."

I tried to comprehend her words. "In short mother, you are caught between your love for Yahweh and your respect for Samaritan customs?" I asked.

"That's one way to look at it, my daughter. The longer we wait for a son, the more tired I become. Perhaps I am losing faith." The sad countenance returned to mother's face.

"You will have a boy, mother. You do not need to be sad. Besides, you can dedicate me to Yahweh. I will serve Him all my life." I wanted mother to always be happy.

"Your words are kind, Marnina. Thank you very much. Just remember always that I love you," mother said, stretching her hands towards me. I accepted the embrace, wrapping my arms around her neck.

The rest of the day was the usual routine. We tidied the house and prepared Father's dinner. I was eager for Father's return and was just about to ask mother why he was late in returning when I heard his footsteps at the door. I ran towards him as he walked tiredly into the front room. "Welcome home, Father."

He carried me into his strong arms and kissed my cheek. "I'm glad to be home, my Rose. It has been a very long day. As soon as I finish dinner, you will tell me all about your dream, won't you."

"Most certainly I will," I said, looking forward to time with Father.

Mother walked into the front room and gave Father a hug. I felt the warmth of the love they had for each other but for a moment wondered why they did not spend more time together. Father always seemed to work and Mother always seemed to cook. Things can be different, I thought.

After supper, Father came into my room, still looking exhausted. "I won't tell you any story tonight my Rose, because I need to go to bed soon. But I will stay up all night if need be to hear about your dream."

"That's alright Father. You'll tell me another one tomorrow." I sat up on my mat and began to narrate my dream.

"In my dream, I saw myself hurrying through a field. I was trying to get away from something but did not feel like I was being chased. The more I ran, the more tired I became. I was also becoming increasingly thirsty. Looking around me I could not find any stream or fountain from which I could refresh myself. I kept on moving further into this endless field until I finally fell to ground out of exhaustion."

"Then what happened next," Father asked, sensing that there was more to the dream.

"I do not know for how long I was on the ground, but suddenly, I felt a strong hand tug my shoulder. I regained consciousness to find a young, fine-looking man standing beside me. He was dressed in white that seemed to reflect the rays of the sun. In his hand was a bowl of water. He offered it to me and told me to drink. I drank hurriedly from the bowl and immediately began to feel revived. Half-way into drinking, the man began to speak to me. He said, 'You are on a journey of destiny. You are looking for something and for someone. The search will end on the day you meet The Greatest Well-digger in the World. On that day, you will find the path to Highest Joy. For this reason you were created, uncover the path of life.'"

"The man had spoken with so much authority. His calmness also gave me a sense of security, the kind of feeling I have when I am with you Father. I was not frightened when I asked him, 'Who is The Greatest Well-digger in the World and where can I find him?'"

The young man dressed in white smiled and said, 'Become a friend of the Torah and you will one day meet him at Jacob's well'"

As I closed my eyes and pondered on those words *The Greatest Well-digger in the World,'* I suddenly became aware that I was speaking with an angel. I slowly opened my eyes only to find that the young man in white had disappeared. I looked all around the field from where I was sitting and he was nowhere in sight. At that moment I woke up and realised I had been dreaming. Not only was it quite vivid, I could remember every detail of the dream."

Father was listening intently all the while. When I finished narrating the dream, he just sat there, as if he was in a trance. Then slowly, he started to mutter, "The Greatest Well-digger in the World."

After the third time, Father asked me to describe the young man dressed in white, and I went through the man's features again. The more I described him, the deeper Father seemed to be lost in thought.

Then Father started to nod his head. "What is it Father?" I enquired. "Do you know what the dream means?"

"No, I don't understand the dream yet, but I have seen the young man before," Father said, still nodding his head.

"You have? Where?" curiosity and excitement were building up in me.

Father looked straight into my eyes and said, "He is the same man who appeared to me in my dream to announce your arrival and your destiny. His clothes were glowing and his hair glittering weren't they," Father asked.

"Yes they were," I confirmed.

"He's the same person quite alright. Marnina, Yahweh is watching over your life. You just saw an angel in your dream telling you about your future!"

An angel, I thought to myself. Am I *that* special?

"You are special, Marnina. Yahweh has plans for your life. Your love for stories, your rich imagination, your pleasant nature, all these are part of the precious gifts He has endowed you with. You must know at all times that you are special in

Yahweh's sight. Remember what the angel told me about you?" Father's eyes brightened as his questioning eyes stared at me. I could only nod my head in agreement.

"Your life will be a blessing to many in Samaria. Always remember that," Father said, holding me close to himself.

At that moment, Father was to me the angel that was watching over me. He was always encouraging and affirming me. Through his eyes, I could only see myself as a special person.

Will I truly be a great woman in Samaria? What about the prevailing custom that subdued and undervalued women? What about the perception of society? What was I running away from in my dream? Why was I exhausted and thirsty? And who is The Greatest Well-digger in the World?

Father noticed my countenance and said, "Are you alright, Marnina? I know all this can seem too much to you."

"I am fine Father. I just don't know what the angel meant by The Greatest Well-digger in the World. Do you, Father?"

Father's countenance dropped slightly. "No I don't, not yet. But we will find out and you will meet him just as the angel said. In the same way I was directed to read the Torah, so have you. I think the words of Yahweh have an answer for us. Just give me a few days and I hope to have something to tell you about The Greatest Well-digger in the World."

I knew he would. I only had to endure the torture of waiting.

"Thank you Father. I can trust you at all times."

5

Waiting is not something a child does very well. "A few days" seemed to last forever. I was eager to know who 'The Greatest Well-digger in the World' was. Father promised he will find the answer in the Torah, and Father always kept his promise.

Father loved Yahweh and was always keen on learning more about Him. He was committed to teaching me all he knew as well. It would worth the time waiting to learn about 'The Greatest Well-digger in the World.'

The day finally arrived. Father came into my room early in the morning. He had an excited look on his face that said, "I have something to tell you! I think I've cracked it," Father said with a smile.

"Cracked what?" I asked innocently.

"A clue about 'The Greatest Well-digger in the World.' I know, at least, the lineage he will come from."

"Tell me Father," I said, eagerly expecting what he had to say.

"I believe 'The Greatest Well-digger in the World' will come from the lineage of well-diggers," Father said.

The blank look on my face must have said it all.

"This is what I mean. The Greatest Well-digger in the World will be a descendant of Abraham, because Abraham was a well-digger, his son Isaac was a well-digger and his grandson Jacob was a well-digger too. The Greatest Well-digger in the World will certainly be part of that family line."

I honestly did not understand what Father was saying, but he looked like he knew what he was talking about.

"Don't worry about the details now, my Rose. I will tell you more about it when I come back from the farm."

"No Father, tell me now," I protested.

"You know I can't, Marnina. I promise to tell you more in the evening. Then you can ask all the questions you want. Is that ok?"

It was not ok, but I nodded to say it was. I did not have any choice. Moreover, evening time is not too long a wait and Father always kept his promise. "I will wait Father. Come back home soon."

"I will," Father said as he rose to his feet. He kissed

me on the forehead and said "I love you Marnina. Do have a good day and take care of your mother."

As he walked out of my room, I felt drawn towards him. I ran after him and held his hand. Father knelt down and pulled me to himself. He gave me a big, warm hug that seemed to last forever. I wanted him to stay.

"I will be back," Father said. "You don't need to worry."

"You are my angel, Father," I said, with tears of love welling up in my eyes.

"Don't cry my Marnina. I will not be long today. I promise."

"I will wait for you Father," I said as he walked out of the door and left for the farm.

6

If only I knew how the day was going to end, I would have insisted Father stayed at home. But only Yahweh knows the future and He chose not to reveal the misery that was waiting at our doorstep.

Maybe he did but I was too young to understand. After all, I did not want Father to leave for the farm. Was that my love for him or the God of our fathers trying to prevent foreseen danger?

Mother and I had just finished our lunch when there was a frantic knock on the door. The visitor, who happened to be uncle Eban, Father's younger brother, did not wait for an answer. He swung the door open and called out for Mother.

"You have to follow me now," uncle Eban said. "Something bad has happened in the farm. Follow me now. You have to come too, Marnina."

Uncle Eban did not give any explanation, but the panic on his face was enough to trigger my imagination. All manners of thoughts were going through my head. What had happened in the farm? Has Father been involved in an accident? There was no time to figure out the answers. I ran out of the house and followed close after mother, who was barely catching up.

Uncle Eban spoke very little on the way. When mother asked what the matter was, all he said was "my brother wants to see you both urgently."

This is scary, I thought. Why could Father not wait to see us in the evening as usual? Besides, he had promised to come home early. My mind was busy searching for answers.

As we approached the farm, I could see some people congregated under a tree. I tried to spot my Father's tall and handsome frame among to crowd, but my view was blocked by some of the trees that lined the path. *He is probably behind those two men,* I thought to myself.

When we got close enough, the crowd of men divided to form a passageway for us, and there was my Father lying on the floor, eyes closed.

Mother dropped to her knees beside Father. "What happened? What happened to my husband?" she demanded.

Uncle Eban tried to calm mother down as he explained. "We were all working the fields when suddenly, without any warning, my brother clutched his chest and called out for help. Before we could get to him, he fell to the ground gasping."

"My husband, my husband!" Mother started to cry.

I seemed to freeze on a spot beside Father. Tears were streaming down my face. I just could not believe what was happening. Surely Father is not dead, or is he?

Uncle Eban then said, "I came to call you because before my brother became unconscious, he was calling out your names."

This could not be. Father will wake up when he hears my voice. He most certainly will. I moved close to him and called out, "Father… Father… It's me Marnina. Please wake up." There was no movement from him which made me very scared. "Father!" I tried again. "Please talk to me, Father wake up!"

I paid no attention to the gathered crowd. I had to speak to Father, my angel. "Father!" As I called him for this time, his eyebrows began to move slowly. There was also some movement in his hands.

"My husband," said Mother, holding Father's hand. As I called him again, he opened his eyes and with much effort he responded. "Marnina, my… daughter."

'Yes Father, I am here."

"You will…" Father struggled to say something to me in a voice that could barely be heard. "You will…

one day meet him… The Greatest Well-digger… in the World. When you do… everything will be… alright… You will… find the path… to… Highest… Joy… You will…" Father drew his breath as he tried to continue talking to me, but when he opened his mouth, no words came out.

When Mother started to cry again, it dawned on me that my angel was flying away. I had to go with him. I too can fly. The last thing I remembered was my body slumping on top of Father's motionless chest. My Father had died, and so did I.

7

I opened my eyes and recognised the familiar setting of my room. Looking around from the bed, I spotted the paintings on the wall and the water jar in the corner. Something though, was missing. Someone special. "Father!" I called out.

It was Mother that came through the door. She had a towel and a bowl of water in her hands. "Are you alright, Marnina?"

"Where is Father?" I asked. Mother started to cry. I had been unconscious for nearly two days since Father died and Mother had been afraid she would lose me too. When she did not answer, I faintly recalled the events on the farm. "Is Father really dead?" innocently denying the obvious.

"Yes my daughter. Father is not coming back again. He will watch over us from heaven," Mother said, stroking my head.

I wanted to say something but the words did not

come out of my mouth. I became numb. *Why did I not die with him?* I asked myself. *Why did Father leave me behind? And why did Yahweh allow this to happen?* I could only stare at mother with my teary eyes. Things will never be the same without Father.

Mother asked if I would eat but I was not hungry. She finally prevailed over me and gave me something to eat. I did not speak a word to her. I could not.

I gradually lost interest in everything and only did the basic routines of life. This went long after the customary mourning period.

A part of me died with Father. There were no more stories to listen to and none to tell. To whom can I tell them? Who would care enough to listen? What about all the promises about a great life? *There can be no greatness without Father*, I told myself many times.

It was late one night, just before I drifted to sleep, that I remembered Father's last words: "You will one day meet The Greatest Well-digger in the World. When you do, everything will be alright..." Who on earth is this person?

I also recalled portions of the dream I had. What was the meaning to my dream and the words of the young man Father called an angel? I had no strength to think. I was very exhausted. The greatest man in my life had gone and I was not ready to look for another.

More weeks went by with little or no change in my attitude to life. I hardly spoke to Mother. I also did not eat a lot. My frame became frail and my countenance sad. I slept most of the time hoping not to wake up alive.

It was in the fourth month after Father's death that something weird happened to Mother and me. That word *custom* came to add more sorrow to our already sour lives. It was a custom that would haunt me for the rest of my life. Mother tried to explain but I just could not understand it. How can uncle Eban become my new father?

"It is the law of Yahweh and the custom of our land," mother once said. The more she explained, the more confused I became. "The Torah teaches that when a man dies without a son, his widow must not marry outside the family. Her husband's brother shall take her and marry her and fulfil the duty of a brother-in-law to her. The first son she bears shall carry on the name of the dead brother so that his name will not be blotted out from the land."

I could not believe what mother was suggesting. Uncle Eban to become my father? What kind of tradition is this! Am I not a heir to my Father's inheritance? Has mother forgotten the story of Zelophehad's daughters and that Father had a dream concerning me?

"This is not right mother. Uncle Eban is not my

father!" I protested strongly.

"Daughter, we have no choice. We have to follow the custom of our land. Only a son can continue the lineage of your father. The Zelophehad story applies only to Jews and not to us Samaritans," Mother defended her position with a note of helplessness in her voice.

It was clear to me that mother was resigned to conforming to custom. No wonder why Father's dream never had a positive impact on her. Father believed I was special but mother always wanted a son. I felt unwanted. I felt angry. I felt like running away.

To make matters worse, we were going to leave our house, the place I had known to be home for the last nine years, and move to Uncle Eban's house. I hate custom! I would never subject myself to the cruelty of tradition! Why is there one rule for the Jews and another for Samaritans? How can my Father's brother become my father? It is not fair!

I was convinced life could never get any better, definitely not in Uncle Eban's house. In the middle of sobs, I called out to the air, "Father, why did you leave me to suffer this much, why?" Eventually, I cried myself to sleep, half-consciously contemplating a plan to escape the misery.

8

I woke up early the following morning with much sorrow in my heart. It felt like I had cried all night. There was no sound in the house which made me conclude that mother was not yet awake. Surely, it was too early to journey through unfamiliar paths. Besides, it was still dark.

My thoughts went over the events of the last few months. Father had always been there for me. Now he was no more. Perhaps the angel was wrong. What good can come out of me in the absence of Father? The harder I tried to figure it out, the more hopeless my life seemed. Running away was the only solution I could think of—if I did not want to end up in Uncle Eban's house.

Deep in thought, I heard the sound of mother's footsteps. I also caught a glimpse of the breaking dawn. It is time, I said to myself.

I rose from the bed, stretched my stiff body and

braced myself for my self-imposed pilgrimage. I was too confused and too young to think it through. Where would I go? What danger could happen on the way? I really did not care. The depression of my soul was too dense for clear reasoning.

I was going to look at mother's face for one more time. Even though I would miss her, the sense of loss I already felt overshadowed any further bereavement. I preferred to be dead myself.

I met mother in the front room and greeted her. This surprised her as she had been the one to first greet me since Father's death.

"Are you alright this morning," mother enquired, placing the back of her palm on my neck.

"Yes mother," I said, managing a weak, brief smile.

"Daughter," mother continued, "I know you were upset yesterday. But everything will be fine. Besides, you will have someone to cheer you up, someone to play with." She was referring to uncle's daughter. She too was an only daughter, which meant uncle also wanted a son. This whole thing is a mess, I thought. I nodded my agreement but kept my mind on my extradition.

* * * * *

I went outside into the front yard. Mother must have thought it was the usual morning routine of rinsing my face with water. I had other plans. Looking around to make sure no one was close by, I quietly made my way towards the path that led to the unknown. The sky was still dim but there was enough light from the dawn for me to see the clear path.

Slowly, I moved away from the house. My pace gradually increased and soon after, I was running as fast I could. I was convinced no one heard me and I did not look back to find out. I ran and ran, taking this turn and then the other. The only thought on my mind was that of getting away from my pain and the cruelty of tradition. Would my plan work? There was no time for me to think. This was the only logical thing to do.

I did not know for how long I ran. Neither could I recognise where I was. I had stopped running when my feet got tired and had walked for a considerable length of time. Tired and panting, I looked for somewhere to rest. There was a tree nearby. As I moved closer to sit under its trunk, I started to cry. I sobbed for a long time. The pain of my heart was like a big lump in my chest. Surely, I was doing the right thing. Or, was I? I could no longer tell.

The confusion made my heart fear. I also began to feel hungry. Looking over my shoulder in the direction I had just come, I thought for a moment about going back home, but quickly dismissed the thought. The real solution would be going *away* – to the place where Father went.

I sat under the tree for a long while, resting my face on my knees and covering them with my hands. I sobbed my heart out in desperation. *Why did Father leave me behind?* Just then, I felt a tap on my shoulder.

Surprised and scared, I looked up and saw the figure of a man in white clothes. I wiped my teary eyes for a better view. For a moment I thought I had seen the young man before. It was when he called me by name that I realised who it might be.

"Marnina," the young man said, "weep no more."

It was the angel I had seen in my dream! The same one Father had seen in his dream. I could feel the aura of his presence around me. His white garment sparkled with light. *Has he come to tell me why Father died? Is he going to take my pain away?*

"You are in anguish today," the angel continued, "but your heart will be healed tomorrow. The day you meet The Greatest Well-digger in the World, you will learn the keys to Highest Joy…"

Not again, I thought to myself, unaware of what the angel was saying. *Who is this person I had to meet before happiness returns to my life? Where is he? Why must I meet him before my life can turn around?*

"You have many questions, my daughter," the angelic voice interrupted my thoughts, "but the answers are in the Torah." And before I could open my mouth to query the angel, he added, "Go back the way you came and be a daughter to your uncle."

I looked over my shoulder. Go back? Be a daughter to my uncle? I turned to protest to the angel but to my amazement, he was no more there! I glanced my left and then my right. Where is he? I thought. Rubbing my eyes with my shaky hands, I hoped it was all a dream.

The brief encounter left me anxious. Questions began to form in my head. Who is The Greatest Well-digger in the World? This was the biggest question of all. What will the Torah reveal concerning this mystery?

In spite of the uncertainties, the angelic visit gave me the impression that Yahweh knew about my plight. If only He told me why Father died, not that any answer would satisfy. Can I trust Him? Somewhere deep within me, I resolved to do just that. I had to for Father's sake. If Father trusted the words of the angel and loved the Torah, perhaps I should too. Moreover, Father believed enough to love me even though I was not a son. His dream set him free from the traditions that kept mother unhappy. For his sake I would try to believe.

I rose to my feet and braced myself for going back home. The tiny glimmer of hope within me did nothing to prevent the dread of returning. What would mother say? How would uncle Eban react? Will I truly make it without Father?

Slowly, I began to walk away from the place of my

encounter. I looked back and then looked around. Everything was bare. The little ray of hope was not under the tree or in the horizon; it was somewhere deep inside me. *Father, please guide me home*, I prayed silently.

Just then, I heard a sound in the distance. I looked in the direction of the sound and saw some people heading my way. At first, I could not recognise any of them but as they moved closer, I saw her. Mother had her hands on her head and was calling out my name. Beside her was Uncle Eban with others behind them. They had been looking for me all morning.

9

"I know this is hard for you," Mother said when we got back home. "I miss your Father too. But we have to continue with our lives. That is what he would want us to do. We must also prolong his family name through his brother."

I knew what she meant but did not like the sound of it. Why does mother have to live up to tradition all the time? I wanted to tell her about the encounter with the angel, but the words could not leave my mouth. Besides, what difference would it make? Would she believe me? Would she believe the angel? I remembered the words: "Go and be a daughter to your uncle." It would not be easy but I was ready to give it a try.

I touched Mother on the shoulder and managed to say a few words. "I will go Mother, and I will not run away again."

She gave a smile of relief and pulled me to her

bosom. "Let us go outside and meet your Father's brother. People are waiting to take us to our new home."

Two people were standing beside the donkeys that would take us to Uncle Eban's house. They had concerned looks on their faces. "Is she alright now?" One of them asked mother. "I think so," she replied.

The other person motioned for us to join the carriage that would take us to the other side of town where uncle Eban lived. I wondered what kind of relationship we were going to develop.

The journey was quiet. When we finally arrived, we were met by some family members and well-wishers. They greeted us warmly and ushered us into the house. It was similar to our old house in design, with its big front room and inner rooms.

I was allowed to wonder around while mother was kept in one of the rooms. Uncle Eban was not in the house and he did not arrive until evening. Mother stayed in the room all this time. When he finally arrived, prayers were offered to Yahweh for the new home and uncle Eban went into the room where mother was. The relatives that were attending to mother vacated the room and left both of them.

Even though I was cared for by attendants, I could not stop myself thinking about Father. I also thought about the angel who appeared to me. I ruminated over the mystery man I am supposed to meet; the mystery man that dug wells for a living. When will I meet him and how will my life change when I do? I restrained myself from slipping into fantasy land. But I could not help thinking whether I would one day get married to The Greatest Well-digger in the World! *You are not ready for marriage,* I told myself. *You are too young!* Well, perhaps I will get married at a young age, I replied myself.

That night, mother and uncle stayed together in the room. I stayed with my thoughts and memories, desperately hoping that everything will work out according to Yahweh's plans.

10

I do not know why I woke up crying, but for the next seven years of my life it seemed to be a daily experience. Deep within me, I could not see the light at the end of the tunnel. I was lost in the middle of nowhere. I was looking for something but had no idea what it was. The feeling of emptiness grew daily.

I tried so much to adapt to my new family but it was not easy. Uncle Eban was not Father. He never told me he loved me. He did not tell any stories. I, too, had not told anyone a story since Father died.

Mother, on the other hand, was learning to be the wife of another man. She did not have much time for me. She really did not know what to do with my moods. She could not see through the dark clouds that enveloped me.

The feelings of isolation escalated when two years after moving to uncle Eban's house, mother gave birth to a baby boy. All the attention was diverted on him and mother's misery seemed to disappear overnight. This is what she wanted all along, a son who will carry the family's name. This is what Uncle Eban wanted as well and he did not try to hide it. I learnt afterwards that he was always at loggerheads with Father because of the love Father had for me. This increased my hatred for the traditions that subjected me to a substandard and second-rate existence.

If only I could meet The Greatest Well-digger in the World! Would he be bound to tradition like everyone around me seems to be? Would he be like Father who lived by the words of the angels and knew freedom from customs and societal expectations? Would he love me like Father did? Would he help me rediscover the joy I once knew? Would he marry me? This mystery person became my daily preoccupation.

Nothing else around me was worth living for. The words of the angel were the only hope I could cling unto. Little by little, I built a world of ideals in my imagination. I began to live in two extreme realities; one where I was not wanted and another where I was loved and celebrated.

In my inner world, I had become what my Father believed was my destiny. Full of joy. Always telling stories. Inspiring both young and old. How I longed for the day! But things were different in the real world. I was the despised slave of an uncaring family.

The only moments I enjoyed were the pockets of time that allowed me to slip into my secret world.

I also looked forward to the usual trip to Jacob's well located at the edge of town. Was that not where the angel said I would meet The Greatest Well-digger in the World?

The journey to Jacob's well was an excuse for me to leave the house. I would rather go to fetch water miles away from home than endure the neglect of my family. The long walk afforded me time to reflect. Father believed the angel's word and showed me love. He said I will be a great woman in Samaria but according to the angel, this prominence is linked to The Greatest Well-digger in the World. I was also told that the mystery was contained in the Torah, which I had not actually paid much attention to since Father died. He was the one who taught me about Yahweh and His laws. Uncle Eban did not, neither did mother.

In spite of my nonchalance, I could still recall some of the stories Father had taught me. In fact, they had recently been coming back to me in logical progression. I remembered Father say before he died that The Greatest Well-digger in the World will come from a particular lineage. He will come from a descendant of well-diggers. Our father Abraham was a well-digger; his son Isaac was a well-digger; and his grandson Jacob was a well-digger. The evidence has lasted many generations. Who can be greater than these great well-diggers? I mused on the thought for many weeks.

In my thinking, no-one can exceed Jacob when it came to well-digging. Abraham was great and Isaac was wise. But for Jacob's well to survive till today was an awesome achievement. There can be no-one greater! Perhaps the angel was mistaken!

Usually, I would think on these things on the way to the well and all the way back. I hardly spoke to anyone lest I break the trend of my thoughts.

But the day came when all that would change.

11

"My name is Marnina." The words came out of my mouth before I could gather myself to ask why he asked or who he was.

"I had been watching you come to the well for some time and today I summoned the courage to approach you. My name is Gabai, a Samaritan from the region of Janin." His eyes were fastened on mine as he spoke. His tender voice eased any fear that I could have had.

"Watching me?" I queried.

"Yes. I have been working in Sychar for a while and I usually walk down this path most mornings. You probably have not noticed me, but I did you. It is hard to forget a beautiful face when you see one," he said with a gracious smile on his face.

Did he just call me beautiful? Father was the last person who said that to me. Who is this man and why is he interested in speaking with me?

"Sorry I did not notice you. I am usually in a world of my own when I come to the well." Momentarily, I felt guilty for ignoring everyone around me. I had done this for so long that it felt like the right thing to do. How else could I cope with an unloving society bound by a cruel tradition that disadvantaged women?

"You need not apologise," Gabai said. "I am sometimes like that myself."

Suddenly, I began to feel tense inside me. I felt like running back home, for what reason, I was not sure. Gabai broke the short moment of silence and said, "Do you come to the well everyday?"

"Most days," I replied, trying to hide my uneasiness.

"Can I meet you here tomorrow," Gabai asked, looking into my eyes. I nodded in the affirmative and told him I had to go. As I turned to face the direction that led home, Gabai said, "I will be waiting for you here tomorrow."

My heart began to pound. I could not stop it from racing faster than normal. *Calm down, Marnina,* I kept telling myself as I paced home. I spilled half of the water before I finally reached the front door.

"Are you alright?" Mother asked.

"I am, Mother, just a bit dizzy." Wanting some time alone, I went straight to my room and lay on the bed. Why did I suddenly become nervous? There was something about the man that triggered my edginess.

He had a voice like Father. Come to think about it, he looked a bit like him; perhaps a bit taller and darker, but certainly the same eyes and hair pattern. Then, he called me beautiful. I had not heard anyone speak so tenderly to me for ages. Tears welled up in my eyes as sweet memories flooded my mind.

I had to run away because so many things were being stirred within me. The most intriguing was the prediction of the angel. Was it about to come to pass? I wondered what kind of profession the fine-looking man did. After all, he said he was working in the region. Does he live in this town or is he from another? Is he married? Does he have children? Could he be the one I am destined to meet, the one who would usher me into Highest Joy? I wanted to see the stranger again. I could not wait for morning to come.

* * * * *

I got up earlier than usual the following day. My mind was fixated on the previous day's meeting. In a little while, I was going see the stranger again. I *wanted* to see him again. I wanted to ask him a simple question.

Assuring mother that I felt better, I began to make my way to the well. For the first time in a long time, I took particular care in the choice of clothes I wore and how I looked. This could be my turnaround day, I thought.

The journey seemed quicker than usual. In the

distance I could see the well. As I moved closer, I spotted the man, already waiting for me. I slowed down and calmed my nerves. I really did not know what to expect. What if he *is* a digger of wells?

The man saw me and made his way towards me. He bowed slightly and said "Hello beautiful one."

"Good morning," I managed to reply.

"I could not wait to see you again, Marnina. I thought of you all through the night." Gabai's eyes were fastened on mine. I looked away not wanting to admit that I was thinking of him too.

"Are you heading for work today?" I asked, wanting to get to the root of my enquiry as soon as possible.

"Yes I would, after a little while with you," Gabai said, smiling. I will join the rest of the family later at the other edge of town."

"You have family here in Sychar?" I asked curiously.

"Yes. There are five of us with our father, five brothers. Mother died a few years ago," Gabai revealed.

"I am sorry to hear that," I empathised.

"Thanks. It has not been easy since she left, but we have continued the family business which is what brought us to Sychar."

This was my opportunity to find the answer to the

question burning in my mind. I wanted to know if this fine-looking man is the predicted well-digger. I drew a short breath and asked, "And what is your 'family business'?"

Unaware of my keen anticipation, Gabai casually said, "Ours is an unusual business. We are a family of well-diggers."

Just like the previous day, I froze on the spot, only that this time, I did not want to run away.

"Professional well-diggers?" I asked. I could not believe my ears!

"Yes. My father and brothers work together for a wealthy old man," Gabai explained. "Together with other servants of his we have dug four wells in the last few years."

"So you are a well-digger," as if I needed another confirmation.

"Yes Marnina, so is everyone in our family," Gabai restated, unaware of what was going on inside me.

Is this it? Is this The Greatest Well-digger in the World? I studied Gabai's features. He was tall and well-built. His eyes sparkled with life. His voice was gentle and soothing. Somehow, my mind told me he was the one. I could not wait to find out any further. This could be the man of my dreams!

I smiled as he told me about his family. His father was a very religious man, a worshipper of Yahweh, who had taught his children to fear the Almighty. Many times in the year they all went up the mountains of Samaria to worship. His mother died four years ago. She was a homemaker who also taught them to be responsible men in society.

Before I knew it, I was talking about myself and my family. Gabai's calm presence was a comfort to me as I slowly opened the wounds of the past and talked about my Father and how much I missed him. I was close to tears but not bitter like before. Gabai gently touched my shoulder as if to say, "Do not cry, everything will be alright."

"You remind me of Father," I said, wiping the tears that were welling up in my eyes.

"Come to think of it," Gabai said, "you remind of mother too. And how I miss her so!"

There was a moment's silence that seemed to go on forever. I think our souls met and touched each other in that instance of recognition.

"Would you be here tomorrow?" Gabai said, realising the time we had spent already. "I will like to see you again."

"You can be sure of that," I replied.

The angel was right. I have met the fulfilment of prophecy, the man of my dreams. This is the turnaround I have been waiting for. The Greatest Well-digger in the World would lead me on the path to Highest Joy.

But would he ask my hand in marriage? If he did, I knew what my answer would be. I concluded there and then it was only a matter of time.

12

When you've lived in dream land for such a long time and suddenly your dreams threaten to come true, all sorts of emotions run wild within you. From anxiety to excitement, disbelief to expectation, I experienced them all. More than these, I felt special, just like Father had always affirmed. Why did an angel have to predict the things I was now living? I discovered the folly of entertaining thoughts of death. If I had taken my life in my hands and squashed it like you would an ant on the floor, there could be no chance of anticipating the reality that had sprung itself on me. Truly, humans are short-sighted!

Gabai is pleasant and good-looking. He is a worshipper of Yahweh and a digger of wells. We met at a well just as the angel had predicted. What else did I need as way of confirmation? Besides, I longed to be with Gabai and he told me the same was true for him.

In the course of time, Gabai brought each of his brothers to meet me at the well. They were all fond of me and talked openly about welcoming me as part of the family.

The day finally arrived when Gabai's father and family elders came to our house to ask my hand in marriage for Gabai. Mother was expecting a second child and could not move around too much. There was ample help for her though. Uncle Eban (which was still the way I regarded him) and the other relatives received the bride price from Gabai's family and we held a party that lasted a few days.

I was glad when the festivity ended, because now I could start my new life with the man I had grown to love in a short time. Gabai promised he will love me always. I believed him. I was ready to be his wife forever too.

13

Becoming the wife of a man who loved me was the best thing that could have happened to me at the time. Before I met Gabai, life had become a journey to endure. Now, I had the chance to enjoy life again. Many of my childhood experiences resurfaced. There was someone who cared for me and constantly affirmed me. Like Father, Gabai was free from some of the traditions that confined many Samaritan men. He loved openly. He made me bud again with the passions that were locked deep within me. One of such was my love for stories!

As busy as Gabai was, he had time to listen to me, mostly at night time. Actually, I heard more from him because, like Father, he loved to talk about Yahweh and had a lot to share from the Torah. There was much I did not understand and I frequently asked Gabai questions.

One particular day, a few months into our

marriage, I sought knowledge about something Father had said before he died. I asked Gabai directly, "Are you a greater well-digger than our forefathers Abraham, Isaac and Jacob?"

Gabai had a puzzling look on his face? "Why do you ask an impossible question, my sweet one? Who can be greater than the fathers of the nation?"

"But you are a descendant of Abraham, aren't you?" I persisted.

"Certainly," Gabai answered, not knowing where I was going with my questions or why I queried him.

"And you are a digger of wells?" I said.

"Yes, I am, but I will not consider myself greater than our forefathers. Even my brothers are better well-diggers than me!" Gabai laughed at his joke, which was not at all funny to me. My husband is supposed to be the greatest well-digger in the world!

"Our forefathers dug wells because they had a land to possess. Well, we are digging wells for a living. There is a world of difference between the too. There cannot be anyone greater than our fathers Abraham, Isaac and Jacob."

Gabai's explanation left me a bit confused. I had not told him about my dreams and the prophecy about meeting The Greatest Well-digger in the World. I could not recall why I had not told him but I was glad I had not. That we were married was more important now. I had married a well-digger and to me he was the greatest in the world!

Gabai soon discovered some unexplored depths in his wife. Not only did I ask many questions, I also told him stories and shared my fantasies. I told him about my dream of becoming a story-teller that would gladden the hearts of people everywhere in Samaria. He thought it was a good idea but wondered how it would come to pass in a society that underrates women. "Only men told stories," he once said. But I was not dissuaded by the reality check. It only served to strengthen my resolve.

Gabai was also devoted to Yahweh. Every year, we would go up to Mount Gerazim to worship with his father and brothers. I learnt a great deal during these trips. I learnt more about the laws of Yahweh and the traditions of my people. I became aware of the different approaches to worship, particularly between Samaritans and the Jews. One thing was common though: we were both expecting the coming of the Messiah. He was coming as a ruler who will liberate the nation from Roman rule and occupation. The expectation amongst the worshippers was stronger than ever before. In fact, there were rumours that a man from Nazareth was claiming to be the Expected One. He is certainly not the first to draw attention to himself. Amongst others, there were widespread stories about a weird prophet baptising people in the Jordan river!

Gabai and I were expecting the Messiah too. But we were consumed in the love we had for each other to give much focus to the longing. *He can come whenever he wants,* I remember thinking one day. Something inside me was kicking against tradition and custom. Everyone in Samaria can spend their time looking forward to a deliverer from heaven, I will concentrate on loving my well-digger husband. I did not want tradition to take that away from me.

Perhaps I was wrong to love Gabai this way – over and above Yahweh's messenger. Was that what Yahweh saw in my heart that made Him send His terrible east wind to blow angrily upon the tender plants in our love garden? Had I broken the golden rule that required me to love the Lord with all my heart, soul and strength? It has taken me a lifetime to come to terms with what began to happen in my life next.

14

It was a morning like every other, but on this fateful day, I woke up early and puzzled. My mind was troubled by a matter I could not comprehend. I realised it was the dream I had just before dawn that was troubling my mind. I remembered it vividly but could not understand its meaning. My face went pale and I could not hide it from Gabai.

"Why are you downcast this morning, my Sweet One?" Gabai asked. "Are you having a headache?"

"Not a headache, my husband," I replied. "I am troubled by the dream I had this morning."

"Come share it with me," Gabai said, holding my hands in his and leading me to a mat on the floor. "Perhaps Yahweh will give us insight into its meaning."

We sat opposite each other. I could not stop my body from shivering even though the house was warm. "Try and calm down, my sweet one. There is

no mystery under the sun that Yahweh cannot solve."
My husband encouraged me to share the dream.

"I was walking down a familiar path alone," I
managed to begin. "It seemed like I was heading for
an unknown destination. The more I walked on the
path, the less familiar it became. Then suddenly, I
became aware of someone walking with me. When I
turned to look, it was you, my husband. We walked
on together, chatting all the way. We were happy.
We enjoyed each other." I paused and bowed my
head, evidently shaken by the dream.

"Go on, Marnina. What happened next?" my
husband prompted.

"Then... then your voice became faint, as if you
were talking from afar, a few yards behind me. As I
turned to look, you were no longer there. Instead, it
was the angel I had seen in a previous dream. He
looked into my eyes and smiled. Then he handed me
a stone and said, 'There are six more stones to gather
before you reach your destination.' Out of
desperation, I cried out and said, 'But where is my
destination?' The angel smiled as he said, 'Highest
Joy. Your destination is Highest Joy. You must keep
on going and not look back.' After that, I woke up.
My husband, what does the dream mean?" My voice
was shaking our of fear.

Gabai looked worried. His silence frightened me
more than the dream itself. "What does it mean, my

husband? You are not going to leave me, are you?" I started to cry.

"Of course not, my Sweet One! I will never leave you. You know I love you. I will always be with you. It is hard to interpret the dream, but you know I will always be with you." My husband tried to comfort me.

I knew he was being truthful, but I was still overwhelmed by the dream. How will I survive if something bad happens to my husband? Feelings of grief and destitution began to well up inside me. I wanted my husband to stay with me all day.

"I have to go to my father today. But I will be back sooner than usual."

"Oh no! Please stay! Don't leave me alone by myself," I pleaded.

"My Sweet One, I will be back. Let me just show my face at the family gathering. I will excuse myself and come back home early," my husband insisted.

I could only nod in agreement, even though I was feeling that something was not quite right. In a flash I recalled the day Father left home and did not come back. *My God, please bring him back safely*, I prayed.

15

A frantic knock on the door woke me up from sleep. I had tried to keep myself busy around the house and finally decided to wear time out by sleeping. Who could that be? My husband should be here by now, where is he? Before I could gather myself together, the door flung open and in came my husband's younger brother, the one next to him in age.

"What is the matter? Why are you panting? Is everything alright with father?" In a split second, a rush of dread overshadowed me. *Is my husband alright?* I could not get myself to ask.

Brother Hiram must have seen the concern on my face. "Father is fine," he said. "But Gabai, my brother, is dead."

"What?" I could not believe my ears. My mouth went ajar. It seemed the depth of my soul was about to fly out of me in fright.

"Unknown to us, he was bitten by a deadly snake

on his way to the family gathering. We decided to commence the meeting in his absence, but shortly after starting, a neighbour came in to break the news to us. They had found him lying unconscious on the path that led to the well. We rushed to where he was and found it to be so. We are deeply sorry about..."

I could not think neither could I feel a thing. The last I remembered was dropping to the floor. Brother Hiram was not quick enough to prevent the sudden collapse.

* * * * *

I was unconscious for quite a while. When I came back to myself, I was no more myself. There were a few people in the room where I was lying, both men and women. They all looked sad and gloomy. *Why is everyone miserable?*

One of the women noticed I was awake and came to help me sit up on the mat. Her face was full of grief and sympathy. Suddenly, it all came back to me. *Where was my husband?* The suddenness of the recollection sent me into another shock but this time I remained conscious. *My husband is dead! My husband is dead!* The thought kept reeling in my mind but I could not utter a word.

Why? Why him? Why me? Why us? Why now? Tears began to role down my cheeks. I was not bowling over but I was deeply distressed. It was a long time since I experienced that depth of emptiness. Everywhere inside me felt dark and murky. First it was Father and now my husband. Why does Yahweh do terrible things like this? Why is He bent on seeing me suffer?

Certainly, there was nothing else to live for. I could not imagine life without my husband. He had filled the void left by Father; who will fill the void his death is now creating, a bigger vacuum than the one he filled? Life is full of sorrows and grief!

I refused to eat the food offered me. I just wanted to lie down and sleep. I did not want to wake up alive. I wanted to join my husband in the land of the dead. Why remain on earth when there was nothing to live for? The promised well-digger has come and gone and what am I left with? Every kind of sorrow and nothing near the Highest Joy promised by the angel. And I did not want to see the angel again. I just wanted to quietly leave the world and escape the torture of my many misfortunes. What else could I expect? How much more could I endure?

16

The next seven years of my life was a phase I try not to remember. Memories of those years fail me. How do you live when you do not want to live and yet you cannot die? Yes, I tried to end it all many times and thought about it some more. I merely existed on bare minimum of emotional strength. I could not resist the course of my life. I had no preferences, no dream, no expectation. I was trapped on the road of uncertainty.

It sometimes felt like a force was keeping me alive. Or how else can explain my survival after my husband's? If I saw what was coming next, I would have tried harder to kill myself, or at least, run away. I guess I was living one minute at a time and could not anticipate events, neither could I make any plans for the future.

It was custom, they said. The traditions of Yahweh must be kept. To me, it was ridiculous. It was unfair. But what could I have done? There was no strength in me to resist. After the time of mourning, I had to marry Hiram, my husband's brother.

* * * * *

The day arrived, eight weeks after my husband's death. I cried. I protested. I tried to fight. But I was too exhausted inside. Even mother came to console me. She assured me that it was not as bad as I thought. She was happy with uncle Eban, and saw no reason why I cannot be happy with Brother Hiram. "In fact," mother had said, "he loves you. See how he has been taking good care of you."

Love? Please don't talk about love, I thought to myself. Even if he did, there was no love in me left to give anyone. The loves of my life have been taken away from me one after the other. With what can I love another?

"Well, it is the custom of every God-fearing woman in Samaria," was mother's conclusion, which really irritated me. I had never liked most of our customs and now I was being tormented by the worst of them all. This was a prison sentence I had to endure. I had no advocate and my arguments were weak. There seemed no way out.

I finally surrendered to fate because of a strange thought that entered my mind one afternoon. *Brother Hiram is a well-digger. Could he be The Greatest Well-digger in the World?* I dismissed it as quickly as it came.

I could not believe the thought. *But you are still seeking for Highest Joy, aren't you?*

Where did that come from? The idea gave a faded glimmer of hope but I knew that Highest Joy will forever elude me. Now I really felt trapped. I was confined by tradition and by the angel of my destiny. What else can a helpless woman do?

And so it happened. I became the wife of Brother Hiram. It killed me inside but I was still alive on the outside. I cannot explain how I survived, without feeling, without love. But I did. I tried to die after he lay with me on our first night, but something kept me alive. The quest for Highest Joy was still on. To be honest, I was not searching for it, but I think it was searching for me.

* * * * *

A year and few months into my marriage with my first husband's brother, who was now my second husband, I began to entertain the thought of giving love a chance. *What if life with my second husband would lead to the promised Highest Joy?* It was difficult but I decided to make the effort. After all, he did care for me. I should at least return the kindness.

Looking back, I wish I had not vowed my efforts, because as soon as I changed my responses to my second husband, he became sick. It started as a little headache and, before long, he became bedridden. In less than two weeks, my second husband gave up the ghost. He died.

That was it. I really died this time. I was no more aware of my surroundings. My life ended. I concluded that love and fulfilment were not mine to experience, not for any length of time anyway. Everyone I became close to contacted my deadly affection and died. Nearly everyone. I remember little of those years of despair but I did get married to all of my first husband's brothers!

Custom. Tradition. Bondage of the highest order. Is Yahweh this cruel? Are people this daft? Must we dogmatically carry on doing something when it is obviously not helping anyone? I certainly did not want to continue, but I felt caged. There was nowhere to run. No easy way to die.

17

The women of Sychar visited the well of Jacob in the early hours of the day. The sun was not yet in its full strength and the rest of the day was devoted to other domestic duties. Everyone had a jug to draw water with and an ear to listen to the latest town gossip. I soon became a ready subject of discussion, both on the way to the well and back. And there was much to discuss! Who else in Samaria had married five husbands? Who else is labelled the husband-killer?

My fifth husband, my first husband's fourth brother, did not wait for death to part us. He found a silly reason to give me a bill of divorcement. He hated me and I hated myself. I hated myself for believing a dream. I hated traditions that had no agenda to set people free. I hated the fact that five men had slept with me, drawing precious water from my well. I now felt dry, completely void of any feeling of love.

I abhorred marriage. What difference was there between me and the whore on the street? I could have sold my body to my series of husbands. Would it have mattered? So much for Highest Joy!

After my fifth husband sent me packing, I had nowhere to go. I was not ready to go back home to mother. She had long given up trying to make sense of the mysterious happenings that surrounded my life. I was not welcome in my husbands' home anymore. I needed a drastic solution.

I entertained the thought of taking my life, again, but I was too worn out to try. The only thing I could do was to find someone to house me. A man. And that did not take too long. As drained as I was, men still found me attractive. I had what any man would want and I was ready to exchange it for what I desperately needed – a roof over my head.

So, I do not blame the women of Sychar for talking about me every morning. I probably would have gossiped about anyone with half the woes I had.

My only way of avoiding the women of Samaria was to visit the well of Jacob in the afternoon, when the sun was up in the sky and the women were indoors.

I tried not to go everyday. I did not want my well journeys to be predictable. So far, I had succeeded in avoiding all the women of Sychar. Until one day, when from afar I noticed someone sitting by the well.

I stopped and tried to have a better look, using my hand to keep the sun rays from blurring my vision. Was that a man? What is he doing at the well at this time of the day? I considered turning back and running home. But something drew me towards the well.

I decided on what to do – draw water as quickly as possible and give little attention to the man at the well. Both plans failed.

18

The first thing I noticed about the man at the well was his fine stature. His clothes were brilliantly white and seamless. He was well kept and his appearance was majestic. I also noticed straightaway that he was not from Samaria. He looked like a Jew. We hardly saw any Jews around.

As I walked past him, I nodded my head, as if to greet him. I hoped he did not take any notice of me. He did.

"Woman," I heard the man say behind me, "will you give me a drink?"

I could not avoid him. I also could not suppress the animosity that suddenly began to rise in me. The anger I had towards the traditions that discriminated between Samaritans and Jews, worse still, between men and women; the customs responsible for my miserable life! I tried to respond as politely as I can. "You are a Jew and I am a Samaritan, a Samaritan woman. How can you ask me for a drink? I thought you Jews do not to associate with us Samaritans. You cannot possibly want a drink from someone like me?" That would do it, I hoped. He will leave me alone.

"Woman," he said, evidently unaffected by what I said and *how* I said it, "if only you knew the gift of Yahweh and who it is that asks you for a drink, you would have asked him and he would have given you living water and shown you the path to Highest Joy."

Living water? Highest Joy? Those phrases struck a chord but there was a fight going on in me. My defences were up and I struggled to conceal them. "Sir," I said as politely as I can, "you are certainly no well-digger. You have nothing to draw water with and the well is deep. Where can you get this 'living water' from? Besides, are you greater than our father Jacob, who gave us the well and drank from it himself, as did also his sons and his flocks and herds? You cannot really mean what you have just said."

Instead of getting mad at my rudeness, the man at the well just smiled. His countenance seemed to radiate light. There was a calmness and peace about him. He showed no sign of being repulsed by me. "Everyone who drinks from this well will be thirsty again," the man said in a deep, convincing voice. "But whoever drinks the water I give will never thirst again. Indeed, the water I give will become in you a spring of water welling up to eternal life."

He probably is a well-digger, I thought, *but of a different kind.* His words seemed to silently quell the fight in me and I began to desire the "living water" he offered. "Sir," I implored with hands outstretched, "give me this 'living water' so that I won't get thirsty again and have to keep coming here to draw water."

He must have sensed the desperation in my voice. "So, you do want 'living water' and the path to Highest Joy? Go, call your husband and come back."

I drew my hands back and stood in disbelief. *What does my husband have to do with 'living water' anyway? But I have no husband, not anymore.* "Sorry sir," I said, "I have no husband."

He smiled again as he looked lovingly into my eyes and said, "You are right when you say you have no husband. The fact is, you have had five husbands, and the man you now have is not your husband. What you have said is quite true."

I felt like disappearing into the ground. *The gossip has reached the towns of Israel!* I was staying with a man so I could have a roof over my head. And my five husbands, I certainly did not want to talk about that chapter of my life. This is the reason I fetched water at noon and not in the morning. I had to change the subject.

"Sir," I said, concealing my embarrassment, "I can see that you are a prophet. Our fathers worshipped on this mountain, but you Jews claim that the place where we must worship is in Jerusalem. Why all the confusion? Which is right and which is wrong?"

Even though I was trying to avoid the issue of my personal life, there was something deep inside me that wanted to know how to worship Yahweh acceptably. There were too many traditional practices and customs that did not give a sense of connection with the Almighty. If this man that claimed to know the keys to Highest Joy is really a prophet, he should know which is right and which is wrong. But if he too was bound by tradition, I would not want anything from him, living water and all. I waited to hear how he would handle the test.

The man in white did not lose his peace. "Believe me, woman," he said with a tangible air of authority, "a time is coming when you will worship the Father neither on this mountain nor in Jerusalem. You Samaritans worship as best as you can and so do we Jews. Yet a time is coming and has now come when the true worshipers will worship the Father in spirit and in truth, for they are the kind of worshipers the Father seeks. Yahweh is alive and does not want dead traditions. Yahweh is spirit, and his worshipers must worship in spirit and in truth."

There was something different about this man. His words reached deep down into my soul and seemed to break the shackles of tradition that had held me captive for years. He was not like most Samaritan men I knew. In fact, he reminded me of my Father, a man who did not allow tradition to restrict him. In a flash, I remembered how the angel had helped him to accept me, a female child, and how he loved and affirmed me. I remembered his love for Yahweh and the story times we shared together most evenings. I remembered his firm belief in the coming of the Messiah, the One who would come to teach us the worship of Yahweh and free us from all bondage...

This man in white knew something of Yahweh and spoke with authority, but he certainly cannot be the Messiah, or could he?

I concluded it could not be possible. "Thank you for solving that puzzle for me. Even though it raises many more questions. For instance, what is 'true worship'? Anyway," I said, not wanting to start another lengthy discussion, "I know that the promised Messiah is coming. When He comes, He will explain everything to us."

All the while, the man in white had sat down majestically by the well. This time, he rose to his feet and took a step towards me. He stretched out his right hand and touched my left arm as he said, "Marnina, I who speak to you am He and the water I give you is the Spirit."

19

I was shell shocked! How did he know my name? Is he really the Messiah? My mouth was ajar as I froze on the spot. He just stood there in front of me, ensuring that the sudden awareness gently saturated my heart. And it did, like trickles of dew on a parched and dry land.

I wanted to say something but could not find the words. As I summoned the strength to speak, some men began to approach the well. They came straight where we were, all of them Jews. For some reason unknown to me, I counted the men; they were twelve in number.

"Master," one of them said, "we are back with the food."

He is the Christ! I said to myself. The twelve men, his disciples, further confirmed it to me. Immediately, I left my water jar at his feet and hurried into town. I could not keep this revelation to myself. I had to tell the good news to the elders of the town.

The further I ran, the lighter I became inside. I did not feel any shame as I considered speaking to the elders. The Messiah had unburdened my heart. He knew me by name! He knew everything about me. There was nothing to hide anymore. Yahweh had not abandoned me after all!

I remembered the words of the angel and suddenly it all began to fit together. The Messiah could very well be The Greatest Well-digger in the World! He had offered me living water, "the Spirit," according to Him. He had spoken about wells that would continually flow unto eternal life. He hinted that He knew the path to Highest Joy, the very words the angel had used to initiate a lifelong quest in me. Above all these, He knew me by name! I could not contain myself!

Just then, I saw three of the town elders walking towards the market square. They were shocked to see me running towards them. They hardly saw me outside in the day and most certainly not radiant with such joy.

With much excitement, I began to testify, "Come, see a Man who told me everything I ever did. Could this be the Messiah?"

They looked at me in disbelief. I could read their minds: *everyone knows everything you ever did; how does that make this man the Messiah?* So, I calmed down a bit and told them a bit more. I told them the Man was a Jew and not from Sychar. I described the splendour of His stature and the authority of His words. I narrated the whole encounter and insisted that He knew my life by revelation and not by information.

"He even knew my name!" I said. "Come and check him out for yourselves. He might very well be the Christ."

By this time, more people had gathered and were hearing me speak – more from the surprise of seeing me in the open, I guess. My excitement and the rare boldness with which I spoke triggered enough curiosity in the people. One of the elders motioned to speak. "We all know that Marnina is not usually this full of life. Something has *definitely* happened to her. I think we should go and see the man she is referring to. If he is the Messiah, then the whole town needs what he gave to Marnina."

Everyone nodded their agreement and began to follow me back to the well. There was a spring in my step as I jogged along. I could never have imagined the day I would influence people by *my story*. So much prophecy was being fulfilled in a single day. I just had to go with the flow and see where it led.

When we got back to the well, the Messiah was speaking with the twelve men. The food they bought had not yet been touched. As we drew near, the

Messiah said, "I knew you all were coming. The kingdom of Yahweh has come to Sychar!"

One of the three elders spoke up. "Everyone can see that there is a change in Marnina's life. And she only met you today."

The Messiah smiled as he said, "Whoever sees me and receives the words from my mouth will enter into true life and understand the path of Highest Joy. I came especially for Marnina, but what has happened in her life can happen to each one of you as well if you will believe."

"Please come and stay with us in Sychar," the elder requested. We need to hear what you have to say. A house will be prepared for you and your disciples, as well as food to refresh your body and soul."

"We will stay," said the Messiah.

I was deeply touched when I heard the Messiah say He came especially for me. So, my life does worth the trouble. Was I not tagged a 'husband-killer' and a whore? Was I not a reject in Sychar? Had I not given up on life many times over? But the Messiah knew me and cared for me, even when I had thought that Yahweh was the source of my misery. How fortunes can turn around in a single day!

So, the angel was right all the while. Silently, behind the scenes, he had kept me from ending my life. He preserved me for this very moment, the day of release from bondage.

This Man, Yeshua, is truly the Messiah, the Greatest Well-digger in the World! Actually, I did not fully understand how he was The Greatest Well-digger in the World. I just believed the word of the angel. Somehow, I knew I would understand. I could not wait for the rest of the prophecy. I was eager to learn the path to Highest Joy.

I followed the throng of people accompanying the Messiah into Sychar. With a big smile on my face, I knew my life will never remain the same again.

20

The path to Highest Joy! Seven insights of the kingdom of Yahweh. I have rehearsed them so many times, both to myself and to others. I can recall them, it seems, word for word.

How refreshing were the words of the Messiah in the ears of those who heard Him during His two-day stay in Sychar! He did not speak like the teachers of Samaria who were clogged by their tradition and custom. These were fresh words from heaven; insight and revelation that set the oppressed free.

I was set free from my life misery. Many others experienced deliverance as well, with many of them telling me how blessed they felt after hearing the words of the Messiah.

"We no longer believe just because of what you said," some said to me. "Now we have heard for our-selves, and we know that this Man really is the Saviour of the world."

Although the Messiah stayed with us for only two days, the words that he spoke have stayed with us ever since. He is truly the Greatest Well-digger in the World! That I now know without a doubt. He sought me out and patiently dug out all the dirt that buried my purpose and destiny. He came to release the potential in me. No one else could have accomplished it, no one but Him.

The path to Highest Joy that the Messiah taught us over two days, seven progressive understandings about attaining kingdom joy, reveal why He is the Greatest Well-digger in the World. Oh that the whole of Samaria would embrace these insights and discover the path to Highest Joy! Oh that they would abandon their traditional ways and enter the kingdom of the Most High!

The seven insights that lead to the path of Highest Joy bypass religion and go straight to the heart of God's purpose for His people. I am so glad He chose me to be a recipient and an example of these principles. What Yahweh has now done in me, I pray he will do in others. This is why I tell stories – His stories. I found my destiny when I met the Greatest Well-digger in the World. I learnt from Him the seven keys to Highest Joy and now I am on my way to enjoying abundant life.

Just as the Messiah said on the first day I met Him, I have tasted of His Spirit and inside me is now the wellspring of eternal life. From this depth flows my joy. From this stream flow all the stories I tell. I am now free! Free to be me! Free to help others! Free to glorify Yahweh!

How I wish Father was around today! But it does not matter anymore; he already saw this day; he knew that his daughter will one day flourish for all to see. I give praise to Yahweh for his life. And for the life of my husband; the lives of my husbands. And for my mother, who is still married to Uncle Eban but now appreciates me for who I am. Every experience has prepared me for this moment. I was not aware of it before, but now I know.

I am grateful for everything, the pain and the tears; the ups and the downs. Since I met the Greatest Well-digger in the World and understood the insights that lead to Highest Joy, the adversity of yesterday has become light compared to the ever-increasing weight of glory that is now mine in Yahweh.

I had to go through my unique experiences so that others might find their way in life a bit easier than I did. Yahweh intentionally prepared me for a preordained purpose. I understood it better when Yeshua, the Messiah, showed us the path to Highest Joy. There are no longer any regrets about my past because a great future was open for me—the great future Yahweh planned for me before I was born. I now have a story to tell and a song to sing!

Well, what are these seven insights about Highest Joy that have transformed my perspective about life? What did the Messiah teach the people of Sychar over two days that made such a difference to the whole town? I can just hear Him speaking in my heart, words full of heavenly authority. Everywhere I have recounted them, lives have been changed. As I restate them, I prays yours will too.

21

Insight #1:
Everyone is created by Yahweh with a divine purpose to accomplish in His Kingdom, and unique potential with which to accomplish it.

In the beginning, when Elohim created man, He had a great purpose in His heart for them. This is why He blessed them, imparting in them His blessing, grace and abilities. Everyone who has come into the world since then also has a specific purpose to fulfil in the earth and a proportion of grace with which to fulfil it. No one comes into the world empty. No one comes without an endowment for a particular assignment.

Everyone is unique. Everyone is significant. No two people are the same. There may be similarities between people but, look well and you will find distinctions too. Similarities of gifting call for collaboration in purpose and distinctions call for significant contribution by all. Everyone has something to contribute to life according to each ones' ability. No one is insignificant in the overall plan and kingdom of God.

There is indeed One Purpose to be fulfilled by mankind, One Purpose with many expressions. The Eternal Purpose of Yahweh is for His glory to fill the earth as the waters cover the sea. This is the Vision for His kingdom on earth; His abundance, His peace, His righteousness and His love. Everyone has a portion of the earth to impact with the virtues of the kingdom.

True purpose, therefore, the original intention for placing man on the earth, is the expression of kingdom dominion and heaven's government all over the world.

Until your assignment is fulfilled, this purpose cannot be complete. If you abandon purpose, your portion will not lie fallow forever; it would eventually be given to another to accomplish.

Every God-given purpose, therefore, is important. You have to discover it in your Maker to embark on the journey to Highest Joy.

Responsibility is on parents to help their children discover their gifting and ultimately their purpose in Yahweh. If you train them up in the understanding and use of their gifts, when they grow up they will not depart from purpose. Every child is unique before Yahweh. Of them is the kingdom of heaven.

Your gift is an indication and revelation of purpose. All good and perfect gifts come from the Father above.

The Father gives freely; do not act like you did not receive them.

The Father gives graciously; appreciate the grace that is on yourself and others.

The Father gives intentionally; do not despise your humble beginnings.

The Father gives expectantly; remember you will one day give an account.

True purpose blesses another. True purpose brings glory to Yahweh. Purpose was never meant to exalt self. The one who exalts himself will be brought down to the lowest place of all.

You were fearfully and wonderfully created, carefully designed with some good works to fulfil. Be grateful for your life. Be grateful for your Creator.

The One who created you is watching over you to bring His purpose to pass in your life...

22

Insight #2:
The treasures of purpose are hidden beneath the rubble of life's experiences

Divine purpose cannot flourish maximally apart from the Creator of purpose. When mankind chose the way of sin, Yahweh's purpose for man experienced momentary death, for whatever is alienated from the Author of life is alienated from life. Once purpose was lost, inherent potential had no focus, because purpose is what gives potential direction, worth and meaning.

The potential of man since the fall is buried under the rubble of flesh and sin. From then on, the realisation of purpose as ordained by Yahweh was no more automatic.

There is also an enemy of mankind who further ensures that purpose is not fulfilled and potential is misused. Fearing that purpose may one day be rediscovered and potential channelled aright, he strikes early in the life of unsuspecting humans. The enemy of mankind is afraid of the mighty potential inherent in your gifting and purpose. At the slightest opportunity, he will pile up more rubble on top of the seeds of destiny in you.

If the enemy of mankind does not succeed in killing you, he will mercilessly target the seeds of purpose while they are still small and delicate. He sets man against man, and instigates all sorts of abuse that damages the soul. Adversity, hurts, betrayal, oppression, all these and more are piled on growing souls early in life.

The home was designed by Yahweh to be the place of refuge from the enemy's cruel agenda. Family relationships ought to nurture potential and guard against the destruction of purpose. But a man' enemies are now members of his own household. The time is coming when attacks from within the family will be widespread in the world. This is how far the battle against destiny and purpose has gone and will go.

Ignorant parents will abuse their children and damage their self-esteem. Possessed by wicked spirits, fathers will abuse the innocence of their daughters. Mothers will destroy the confidence of their sons. The burning lusts of man can turn the noblest of souls into brutal beasts.

Upon all these, the pressures of survival is suffocating. Life is not always fair even to the fairest amongst men. Adversity strikes without any warning and without mercy. There is hardly anyone on earth who is not carrying a burden or walking about with life's heave yoke.

Mankind tries with all his might to be free from the burdens of life. Some succeed to a measure, some do not. The memories of failure drain courage out of sincere men. Out of desperation, a man would do anything to preserve his life, even if it means killing another soul, piling sin upon sin. All these take man further away from purpose, piling more rubble on the potential within.

The religions and traditions of men are the rocks that keep all the rubble buried inside a man's soul. Instead of set the seeker free, religion puts man in even more bondage. Religion seeks a way to the Father, a way out of the penalty of death. But there is no other way ordained other than the way of the Son of Man who has come to pay the price for man's redemption.

The Son of man has come to set the captives free and release the potential within. This is the good news of the kingdom, the gospel I have come to declare.

23

Insight #3:
The natural tendency of man is to resign to a life of purposelessness and mere existence

The average man has no hope of fulfilling purpose or becoming great in this life. All he wants to do is live from day to day, and manage to cope with the stresses of living. Potential ends up being underutilised and purpose unfulfilled. Yahweh created man to excel in his place of calling, multiply and fill the earth with goodness. But the average man considers this a tall order to attain. He will rather die in mediocrity than aim for excellence and dignity.

A life without purpose is a life without direction.

A life without direction is a life without a future.

A life without an expectation of a glorious future is a life that merely exists.

Sooner or later, the man who merely exists will begin to

entertain thoughts of putting an end to living altogether. Suicide is never the answer to purposelessness. It only fulfils the will of the enemy of mankind.

Hopelessness is only a momentary state of being, for deep within the soul of the hopeless are the embers of purpose waiting to be rekindled. Under the rubble of past experience lie the gems of future radiance. The average man finds this hard to believe. It is easier to drift along in life than to pursue a distant dream.

The need to survive from day to day is legitimate. The belly needs to be fed and the body needs to be clothed. But if care is not taken, these will become the reason for living and man will cease to live for a reason.

Purposelessness is a contagious disease of the majority of humans. Parents raise children in mediocrity, instilling no motivation for excellence and greatness in them. They overlook budding potential in their children and the purpose for which the Creator has made them. "Man was born to survive and die," they indirectly teach, transferring the curse to the next generation. Vanity, all is vanity. This is the conclusion of man confined to life under the sun. Yahweh, however, created man to rule from realms above the sun. You were not designed to live a life of vanity. You were created to live and experience life indeed!

It requires more than inner strength to ride against the tide of popular mediocrity and enjoy a life of abundance. You were, however, created with and for a great purpose. Never forget this truth.

24

Insight #4:
It takes a man of understanding and perseverance to dig out purpose from another man's heart

It is written in the Volume of the Books that "The purposes of a man's heart are deep waters, but a man of understanding draws them out." Who else understands man better than the Creator of man? Who else knows the potential in man than the One who placed it there in the first place? It does not matter how despondent a person becomes or the pile of sin, bad experiences and pressures that tower over his potential, the Creator still has an eye on the purpose for which man was created. He watches over the words of His mouth and the works of His hands. Even after man gives up on himself, the Creator perseveres because of the value He places on purpose.

Men of understanding who have the Spirit of Yahweh are few on the earth. Most people, even many graciously called into the Levitical Priesthood, will quench a smoking flask and break a bruised reed. But the Son of Man who has the Spirit of Yahweh without measure, will go the extra mile to recover failing potential.

The Son of Man has already come all the way from heaven to the earth. He will yet go deeper into the heart of the earth for three days to redeem the lives and destiny of mankind. He is the Man of Understanding committed to restoring all things, even the original plan of Yahweh for a glorious kingdom on earth.

I have come according to the Volume of the Books, to do the will of Him who created all things for His pleasure. I seek not my own honour but the honour of the One who sent me. I have not come to set up my own kingdom, but to restore the Kingdom that was given to man and the dominion of the King of kings through man. It is because the kingdom of Yahweh is within you, locked up within you, that I have come. I am the Man of Understanding that has come to lay down His life for dying mankind. If you believe in me and partake of me, the wellspring of potential will rise up within you and find its way to the surface — in spite of the rubble that has kept it buried for so long. I am committed to bringing the best out of you. I have the keys that will unlock the treasures trapped within you.

The Son of Man has come to destroy the works of the enemy of mankind. I have come to undo all that the devil has done to confine kingdom purpose. Your destiny can be released if only you will believe.

What religion cannot do, I have come to accomplish.

What sheer effort cannot realise, I have come to manifest. The thief comes to steal, kill and lay waste, but I have come to give life, even abundant life.

Quit struggling on your own. Welcome the Help that has come from above.

Because the Son of Man believes in Yahweh's purpose for your life, you can believe as well.

Because He is full of hope for your future, you can be hopeful too.

Because the Son of Man will face and overcome death, even death on a cross, you can face your tomorrow and conquer any foe.

Whatever and for however long it would take, your purpose in the kingdom will be realised because the Man of Understanding will persevere with you until you overflow with the glory of Yahweh.

25

Insight #5:
Revelation from the Spirit of Yahweh is the instrument for discovering potential and identifying purpose

The Son of Man has come from heaven as the Revelation of Yahweh from heaven. No one has seen the Father at any time, but the Son who came from the bosom of the Father to make Him known. This is the testimony of the Spirit of Yahweh.

Whoever sees the Son has seen the Father who sent Him. Also, whoever sees the Son has seen the True Demonstration of a life of purpose. I am the Demonstration and the Prototype of how the sons of the kingdom ought to live. You are all sons of the kingdom if you follow my example.

Flesh and blood cannot make purpose known to you for these have nothing of value in them to impart to man. The words that I speak they are Spirit and they are life. They are able to take you from where you are into the arena of purpose that was ordained for you from the beginning. The Word was with Yahweh in the beginning, so the Word knows your purpose as it was in the beginning. When I speak unto you, I speak by the Spirit, out of the Volume of that which has been written concerning you. My words touch the heart of your purpose and unveil the reason for your being.

Until the mind of Yahweh is revealed to man, darkness and ignorance will prevail, especially ignorance concerning the events of the past. Yahweh knows the end from the beginning – and all the adversities in between. Even though the enemy of mankind intends for adversity to destroy your potential and thus your purpose, Yahweh uses your past as a fertiliser that nurtures potential and prepares the ground for the fulfilment of purpose.

The stumbling blocks that stand in your way to hinder you today are actually stepping stones that will uplift you to the platform of destiny tomorrow. Revelation from the Spirit of Yahweh will give you this perspective about life and illuminate the paths for your feet.

Your yesterday was preparation for your tomorrow. The comfort that you received in your season of tribulation has equipped you with wisdom to offer comfort to those who are going through the same kind of tribulation.

Have you been abused by others? Yahweh has been preparing you to reach out to others who have been and are being abused. Have you battled and overcome a low self esteem? Yahweh has prepared you to help others who suffer from a low self esteem. Did you grow up in an environment void of love? Yahweh has been preparing you to show love to those who suffer rejection. Your potential and your experience are necessary elements for your purpose.

Allow no one to despise your gifting or belittle your past. All things work together for the good of those who are called to fulfil a good purpose in the kingdom.

When revelation enters the heart of man, so does divine light and the understanding of purpose. Every experience is good when Yahweh's perspective is known.

Now is the time to wake up from the slumber of purposelessness and catch the revelation of Yahweh for Highest Joy. Now is the time to look within and acknowledge the good gifts and the abilities that lie untapped. The Spirit of Yahweh will guide those who are willing into all truth about purpose and destiny.

26

Insight #6:
The identification with and pursuit of purpose in the kingdom is the beginning of the path to Highest Joy

Until purpose is known, the life of man has no real bearing in the kingdom of Yahweh. The light of revelation about purpose places man in his preordained place in the agenda of Yahweh, opening the door to a new lease of life and a new level of service to humanity.

When a person finds his place in the kingdom, every other place loses its appeal. Earthly riches cannot compare with the high calling of purpose. Whatever one achieves outside the parameters of purpose does not count towards eternal reward.

It is good to identify and embrace purpose early, for only one life has been given to man with which he can make an eternal investment in time. Notwithstanding, whenever purpose is discovered is the appointed to embark on the path of Highest Joy.

The place of realisation and identification is the birthplace of passion and zeal that accomplishes feats in the kingdom of Yahweh.

Passion is an indispensable ingredient for kingdom accomplishments. It is a product of wholehearted willingness to obey divine revelation. It is hottest when past experience and innate potential align with the revelation of purpose and a burden to glorify Yahweh in the earth. The host of hell cannot restrain a man on fire for Yahweh!

Absolute obedience to Yahweh's instructions qualifies man for heaven's absolute backing. The authority and resources of the kingdom are available to those who have no agenda of their own to pursue. The man who seeks the advancement of the kingdom of Yahweh with all his heart will have everything else added to his life, even the things that pagan men seek day and night.

The Son of man came to show you how to truly live. Man does not live by bread or for bread alone but by every word and for every word that proceeds out of the mouth of the Father. The words of Yahweh produce faith, joy and true life in those who receive them. Receive, therefore, the word from His mouth and all will be well with you.

The Creator shall one day come and His recompense shall be with Him. He will require from man the fruit of potential. No excuse will be admissible. Only the contributions to purpose will withstand the test and attract a reward. Have this end in view as you live and you will know whether you are truly living. Ignore the day of recompense and distraction will easily lure you to death.

Live your life by laying it down for the purpose of the kingdom. Until you are ready to lay down your life, you are not ready to truly live. You have been called to life, so begin to live out purpose today.

27

Insight #7:
Highest Joy is found in the delight
that purpose produces and the
legacy it leaves in the lives of others,
and its unique contribution to
extending the kingdom of Yahweh

The seeds of potential are not meant to abide alone. When sown into the lives of others, they multiply according to their kind and yield a crop to the glory of Yahweh. This is Highest Joy, living to see the impact of purpose in the lives of others.

The pursuit of purpose produces joy in the lives of those who benefit from it. For this joy, no sacrifice is too much to make; no distance is too far to go. A life of purpose is, therefore, love in action, for love seeks to give and not just receive. "It is more blessed to give than to receive," this is the way of Highest Joy.

Opportunities to give and be a blessing in the lives of

others abound. This reality places a great responsibility upon the sons of the kingdom, for they are called to make the most of life's opportunities and utilise every bit of their ability to better humanity.

Until the end of the earth is touched with all of the seeds of potential that you carry within, there is still more scope for kingdom expression. Of the increase of the kingdom and peace of Yahweh there will be no end, so do not limit the heights you can attain or the lives you can influence for good in this life.

Let your light so shine before men so they can see your good works and give glory to the Father. A lamp only fulfils its purpose when it is set upon a hill to produce light and gladness to its surroundings. It does not matter how big or small the lamp is, it makes all the difference between darkness and light when it is lit. Never underestimate the positive impact your life can make in the life of another.

The least in the kingdom can bless a thousand, and the smallest can impact a whole nation. Such is the plan of Yahweh, to raise a company of kings and priests who will rule the earth and bless the nations. Everyone who believes can be a part for everyone has a part and everyone is a part.

The legacy of the King will last forever. His Kingdom will never end. Anyone can earn the right to rule with Him by living a life of purpose here on earth. The Son of Man is leaving an example for the sons of the kingdom to follow. As the Father has sent me, so send I you. Follow me and you will enter into the joy of the kingdom!

28

The two days that the Messiah spent with us in Sychar transformed the whole town. Many believed in Him and put their trust in His words.

I could not stop weeping for joy as I felt the soothing effect of His healing balm in my heart. His words were life and they gave understanding. The past need not hurt any longer. The rubble has been cleared and potential released.

I pledged my life to purposeful living and resolved to walk the path of Highest Joy. Whatever sacrifice was needed cannot compare with the fruit of obedience. *I am ready, O Lord, I am ready!*

"Marnina," I heard his voice calling me.

"Here I am, Lord," I answered. *He heard my prayer*, I thought to myself.

"Yes, I heard you, daughter of destiny. You can now go free – free from your past and into your future. You will indeed touch many with the wellspring of stories that is in you. Open wide your mouth and I will fill it with wisdom and grace."

"I will go anywhere, Lord. I will do anything," I said, kneeling at his feet.

"From where you are, your fame will go abroad. *Your story* will be told for many generations to come," the Messiah said.

I was about to ask the Messiah about Michael, the man I was living with, when He opened His mouth and said, "The man you have been staying with will ask your hand in marriage. He has received the word and now believes unto eternal life. This will be the next chapter of your life, a glorious chapter with timeless lessons."

I closed my eyes and soaked in the warmth of His presence. He had prepared me and was now commissioning me. "My life I shall live for you, every moment."

The Messiah's hands were on my head as He said, "Go in peace. My grace goes with you."

If you have enjoyed
The Greatest Well-digger in the World
please write the author at:
israel@bwam.org

You can also read
Israel's daily inspirational blog at:
http://www.pastorisrael.com

Get more copies of
The Greatest Well-digger in the World,
The Secret of Abraham
and other inspirational books from
http://www.bwam.org